S. E CHRIS

Fey Flames Of Love

Real Sense
PUBLISHING

Contents

A Witch's Plight

The streets of Arcadia pulsed with restless energy, a tangled web of shadows and secrets that wrapped around me as I moved through the crowds of people. My cloak, a tattered barrier against prying eyes, clung to me like a second skin, concealing the raw power that simmered just beneath the surface. In a crowd of people who had been trained to dread the unexpected, every movement I took felt like a laborious dance, a precise balancing act between fitting in and sticking out.

The king's enforcers lurked in the shadows, their eyes sharp and unyielding as they watched the citizens of Arcadia with a predatory gaze. As I went by, I could feel them watching me, and their presence served as a continual reminder of the threats that could be found in the shadows. I had a mission, a purpose that burned brighter than any fear they could instill.

As I made my way through the winding streets, I couldn't shake the feeling of eyes on me, the weight of their suspicion pressing down on me like a leaden cloak. The ordinary citizens of Arcadia were no different. Their wary glances followed me as I moved past them, their fear of magic a palpable presence in the air.

I gritted my teeth against the whispers that trailed in my wake, the hushed murmurs of suspicion and distrust that threatened to swallow me whole. But I couldn't afford to let their ignorance sway me from my path. I had come too far, sacrificed too much, to let their fear dictate my actions.

With each step, the tension in the air grew thicker, like a suffocating blanket that threatened to choke the life out of me. But I refused to let it consume me. I had a purpose, a destiny that called to me like a siren's song, and I would see it through to the end, no matter the cost.

And so I walked. Through the crowded streets of Arcadia, past the watchful eyes of the king's enforcers, and into the heart of darkness that lay waiting for me. For I knew that I could only hope to emerge into the light by confronting the shadows.

But as I moved through the labyrinthine streets, I couldn't shake the feeling that I was being watched, that unseen eyes followed my every move with a predatory hunger. It sent a shiver down my spine, a cold dread that coiled in the pit of my stomach like a serpent waiting to strike.

I quickened my pace, my heart hammering in my chest as I fought to outrun the shadows that lurked in every corner. But no matter how fast I ran, they were always one step ahead, a constant reminder of the dangers that lay in wait.

And then, just when it seemed like I couldn't go on, a voice cut through the darkness like a beacon of light, pulling me back from the brink of despair. Thalion, the fey prince whose fate had become entwined with mine, stood before me, his eyes burning with a fierce determination that mirrored my own.

"Seraphina," he said, his voice a low rumble that sent shivers down my spine. "We must press on. The fate of our kind depends on it."

I nodded, my resolve hardening like steel as I took his outstretched hand. Together, we would face the darkness that threatened to consume us, and emerge victorious on the other side. For we were not just two souls lost in the night, but warriors bound by fate and fueled by the flames of passion that burned between us.

The twisting streets of Arcadia were covered in a deep fog as we took different paths toward our destination. The air was heavy with the scent of fear and desperation. I moved through the shadows like a wraith, and my cloak pulled tightly around me to conceal the faint shimmer of magic that emanated from my fingertips. Determination burned in my eyes as I pressed on, my resolve unyielding despite the obstacles that lay in my path.

Suddenly, the sound of approaching footsteps shattered the silence like a thunderclap, sending a shiver down my spine. I glanced over my shoulder, my heart hammering in my chest as I searched for the source of the noise. But the thick fog obscures my vision and leaves me vulnerable to whatever threat lurks in the darkness.

With a sinking heart, I realized that I had walked straight into a trap. The king's enforcers surrounded me on all sides, their menacing figures looming out of the mist like specters of death. I cursed under my breath, my mind racing as I weighed my options. There was no way out, no escape from the iron grip of the law that threatened to crush me beneath its heel.

Desperation clawed at my chest as I searched for a way to evade capture, but the enforcers were closing in, their cold eyes fixed on me with unyielding intensity. I clenched my fists, my nails digging into the palms of my hands as I prepared to fight, but a voice in the back of my mind warned me that resistance would only lead to more bloodshed; with a heavy heart, I surrendered to the inevitable, my hands raised in a gesture of defeat as the enforcers closed in around me. But even as the iron shackles clamped around my wrists, I refused to let go of the flickering flame of hope that burned within me.

I knew that no matter how dark the night may seem, there was always a glimmer of light waiting to guide me home. And as I was dragged away into the depths of the city, I clung to that light with all the strength I had left, determined to emerge from the darkness stronger than ever before.

Thalion, the fey prince whose fate had become intertwined with mine, watched from the shadows, his heart heavy with regret. He had sensed the danger that lurked in the path of the street

I followed, but he had been powerless to intervene, his hands bound by the laws of his own kind.

But even as he watched me disappear into the night, Thalion vowed to find a way to free me from the clutches of the king's tyranny. In a world where fear and oppression reigned supreme, our love served as a beacon of light, burning brighter than any darkness. And no matter the cost, Thalion would stop at nothing to see me free once more.

The cobblestones blurred beneath my feet as I sprinted down the narrow alleyway, my breath coming in ragged gasps as adrenaline surged through my veins. The echo of my own footfalls reverberated off the walls, and the iron shackles clamped around my wrists, making a loud noise, a haunting reminder of the danger that pursued me with every step.

My heart hammered against my ribs like a caged bird, its frantic rhythm matching the frantic pace of my flight. The weight of the king's oppression bore down on my shoulders like a suffocating blanket, threatening to crush me beneath its unbearable weight.

With every passing moment, the darkness seemed to close in around me, its icy fingers reaching out to drag me into the depths of despair. But I refused to surrender to the shadows lurking in my mind's corners. I had come too far, sacrificed too much, to let fear dictate my fate.

Just when it seemed like all hope was lost, a narrow gap appeared between two buildings, a sliver of light in the darkness that beckoned to me like a guiding star. Without hesitation, I threw myself through the gap, my body twisting and contorting to squeeze through the narrow space.

I emerged into a narrow alleyway, the sound of my pursuers fading into the distance behind me. For a brief moment, I allowed myself to breathe, the cool night air filling my lungs like a balm to my battered spirit.

But my respite was short-lived, for I knew that danger still lurked in the shadows, waiting for the perfect opportunity to strike. With a renewed sense of purpose, I pushed myself to my feet and set off once more into the darkness, my resolve unyielding despite the trials that lay ahead.

Meanwhile, Thalion watched from the rooftops, his heart pounding in his chest as he witnessed my narrow escape. He had feared the worst when he heard the sound of pursuit echoing through the streets, but seeing me emerge unscathed filled him with a sense of relief unlike any he had ever known.

But even as he watched me disappear into the night, Thalion knew that our trials were far from over. The king's enforcers were relentless in their pursuit, their determination matched only by our own. With a silent vow to protect me at all costs, Thalion leapt from the rooftop and vanished into the darkness, his footsteps echoing off the cobblestones as he set off in pursuit of our shared destiny.

Gasping for breath, I collapsed against the cold stone wall, the rough surface biting into my skin as I struggled to catch my breath. My heart pounded in my chest like a drumbeat, each breath coming in ragged gasps as I fought to calm the storm of emotions raging inside me.

The realization of how close I had come to capture sent a shiver down my spine, the memory of the king's enforcers closing in on me like a nightmare I couldn't escape. I could still feel the weight of their gaze, the cold indifference in their eyes as they bore down on me with all the merciless determination of the law.

But even as fear threatened to consume me, I refused to let it hold me back. I had come too far, sacrificed too much, to let the king's tyranny crush me beneath its heel. With each passing moment, my determination only grew stronger, fueling the fire that burned within me with an intensity that bordered on madness.

I forced myself to stand up and looked around at the barren alleyway in front of me, my hands shaking from a combination of terror and adrenaline. The darkness stretched out like a yawning chasm, its depths filled with untold dangers and hidden perils that threatened to consume me whole.

But I refused to be cowed by the shadows that lurked in the corners of my mind. I had a purpose, a destiny that called to me with a siren's song, and I would see it through to the end, no matter the cost.

With a steely glint in my eyes, I pushed myself forward, my footsteps echoing off the walls as I set off once more into the unknown. There was much danger on the route ahead, but I wouldn't give up. I had allies to find, a rebellion to ignite, and a kingdom to free from the shackles of oppression.

And so, with the weight of the world on my shoulders and the fire of rebellion burning in my heart, I disappeared into the night, my journey just beginning. For I knew that no matter how dark the road ahead may seem, there was always a glimmer of light waiting to guide me home. The cobblestone streets were slick with rain, the sound of my footsteps muffled by the oppressive silence that hung in the air like a pall.

I moved with purpose, my senses sharp and alert as I navigated the twisting alleyways and hidden passageways that crisscrossed the city like a spider's web. Every corner held the promise of danger, every shadow the threat of betrayal. But I refused to let fear dictate my actions. I had a mission, a purpose that burned brighter than any fear could extinguish.

As I moved through the darkness, the weight of the king's oppression pressed down on me like a physical force, threatening to crush me beneath its heel. But I refused to let it break me. I had seen firsthand the suffering inflicted upon the people of Arcadia, the fear and desperation that gripped them like a vice. And I refused to stand idle while innocent lives are destroyed in the name of power and greed.

With each step, my resolve hardened, and my determination to bring about change grew stronger with every heartbeat. I knew that the road ahead would be fraught with danger and uncertainty, but I refused to let that deter me. I had allies to find, a rebellion to ignite, and a kingdom to free from the shackles of tyranny.

With hope burning brightly in my heart, I disappeared into the night, ready to face whatever challenges lay ahead in my quest for justice and liberation. For I knew that no matter how dark the road may seem, there was always a glimmer of light waiting to guide me home. And with that knowledge, I pressed on, my footsteps echoing off the walls as I disappeared into the darkness, my journey just beginning.

The Fey Prince's Burden

The city of Arcadia sprawled beneath me like a vast tapestry woven from shadows and secrets, its cobblestone streets teeming with life even as darkness threatened to consume it whole. From my perch atop the high balcony of the fey court, I watched as the king's enforcers prowled the lanes below, their presence a constant reminder of the oppression faced by magical beings like myself.

My heart weighed heavy in my chest as I witnessed the injustices inflicted upon my people, their cries for freedom drowned out by the deafening silence of the night. I clenched my fists at my sides, the anger boiling within me like a tempest waiting to be unleashed. How long would we be forced to endure the tyranny of the king? How many more lives would be lost before we rose up and fought back?

But even as doubt gnawed at the edges of my resolve, I knew that I could not stand idly by while my people suffered. I had been born to lead, to protect, and to inspire hope in the hearts of those who had none. And though the burden of my responsibilities weighed heavy upon my shoulders, I would not falter. I would do whatever it took to free my people from the chains of oppression that bound them.

My thoughts shifted to the human world outside the boundaries of the fey kingdom as the sun sank below the horizon, illuminating the city in a golden glow. It was a realm shrouded in mystery, a place of wonders and horrors that called out to me like a siren's song. I longed to explore its depths, to uncover its secrets, and to experience firsthand the beauty and cruelty that lay beyond the veil.

But my duties as prince of the fey held me bound to the kingdom, tethered to the responsibilities that came with my station. I could not simply abandon my people to their fate, no matter how strong the pull of the human world may be. And yet, the desire burned within me like wildfire, refusing to be extinguished by the weight of duty and obligation.

With a heavy heart, I tore my gaze away from the city below and turned back toward the palace, the weight of my burdens pressing down on me like a leaden cloak. The road ahead would be long and fraught with danger, but I would not waver. For I am Thalion, prince of the fey, and my people needed me now more than ever.

From my vantage point atop the high balcony of the fey court, I watched with growing unease as a group of enforcers descended upon a young woman, her figure shrouded in the darkness of her cloak. My fists clenched at my sides, the familiar sting of anger coursing through my veins like wildfire. The enforcers' presence in the city was a constant reminder of the king's tyranny, their actions a brutal testament to the oppression faced by magical beings like myself.

I could feel the weight of their gaze, their eyes boring into the young woman with a cold indifference that made my blood boil. But even as rage threatened to consume me, doubt crept into the edges of my consciousness like a serpent coiling around my thoughts. Should I intervene? Should I use my position of power to protect the innocent and uphold justice? Or would my actions only serve to fan the flames of conflict and bring further harm to those I sought to defend?

As I hesitated, unsure of my next move, a voice pierced through the chaos like a beacon of light cutting through the darkness. It was the voice of the young woman at the center of the altercation, her words ringing out with a fire and determination that took me by surprise. Seraphina, they called her, a name as beautiful and fierce as the spirit that bore it.

I leaned forward, my eyes narrowing as I watched Seraphina stand her ground against her oppressors, her defiance a testament to the strength and resilience of the human spirit. At that moment, something stirred within me—a sense of admiration, perhaps, or maybe something more.

For Seraphina was not just another victim of the king's tyranny. She was a symbol of hope, a beacon of light in a world consumed by darkness. As I watched her face down her oppressors with a courage that belied her years, I knew that I could no longer stand idly by and watch from the shadows.

With a determined set to my jaw, I made my decision. I would intervene, not out of a sense of duty or obligation, but out of a desire to stand beside Seraphina and fight for a better future. For she had ignited a fire within me—a fire that burned brighter than any darkness, and I would see it through to the end.

The cacophony of the city streets surrounded me as I descended from my lofty perch atop the fey court balcony. Each step carried me closer to the chaos below, closer to the source of the commotion that had drawn my attention like a moth to a flame. My gaze remained fixed on the figure of the young woman, Seraphina, as she stood her ground against the king's enforcers.

The crowd parted before me like a river parting around a stone, their murmurs of fear and uncertainty mingling with the sounds of my footsteps on the cobblestones. I felt a spark of something unfamiliar stir within me—a curiosity, a desire to learn more about this brave and beautiful stranger who dared to challenge the status quo.

As I drew closer, I could see the fire in Seraphina's eyes, the determination etched into the lines of her face. She was a force to be reckoned with, a spirit untamed by the constraints of society or the expectations of others. And in that moment, I knew that I had to know more about her, to understand what drove her to defy the king's enforcers with such unwavering resolve.

Our eyes met across the crowded square, and for a brief moment, time seemed to stand still. There was an unspoken understanding between us, a connection that transcended the boundaries of race and class. In her eyes, I saw a reflection of my own longing for freedom, my own desire to break free from the chains of oppression that bound us both.

Without a word, I extended my hand to Seraphina, a silent invitation to join me in my quest for justice and liberation. And to my surprise, she took it, her fingers intertwining with mine in a gesture of solidarity and defiance. Together, we stood against the tide of injustice that threatened to engulf us, our hearts beating as one in the face of adversity.

The tension crackled in the air like lightning as Thalion approached me, his steps measured and deliberate. I could feel the weight of his gaze on me, a heavy presence that seemed to linger even when he wasn't looking directly at me. Despite the chaos of the city streets around us, it felt as though time had slowed to a crawl, each passing moment stretching out into eternity.

I watched him through narrowed eyes, my heart pounding in my chest like a drumbeat as he drew closer. There was something about him, something that drew me in despite my better judgment. It was as though we were two sides of the same coin, destined to collide in ways neither of us could predict.

As he reached me, Thalion extended his hand in a silent offer of friendship, his eyes burning with a fierce determination that took my breath away. I hesitated, my gaze flickering between his face and the outstretched hand before me. I knew the risks of trusting a fey prince, knew that our worlds were as different as night and day. And yet, there was something about him, something that called to me in a way I couldn't explain.

With a shaky breath, I reached out and took his hand in mine, the warmth of his touch sending a shiver down my spine. It was a gesture of trust, a silent vow to stand by his side in the face of whatever challenges lay ahead. And though I knew the road ahead would be fraught with danger and uncertainty, I was willing to risk it all for the chance to forge an alliance with him.

Thalion's grip tightened around mine, his eyes locking with mine in a silent understanding. We were two souls bound by fate, destined to walk this path together no matter where it may lead. And as we stood there in the midst of the chaos, our hands clasped together in solidarity, I knew that nothing could tear us apart, for we were Seraphina and Thalion, two hearts united in the face of adversity, ready to take on the world together.

The weight of Thalion's hand in mine felt both reassuring and electrifying, a tangible connection that seemed to bind us together in ways I couldn't explain. Despite the doubts that still lingered in the corners of my mind, I couldn't deny the sincerity that shone in his eyes, the flicker of hope that danced in the depths of his gaze.

With a hesitant smile, I squeezed his hand gently, a silent acknowledgment of the silent vow we had just made to each other. We were two souls bound by a common cause, united in our quest for freedom and justice. And though the road ahead would be fraught with danger and uncertainty, I knew we were unstoppable together.

As we stood there in the midst of the chaos, our hands clasped together in solidarity, a sense of purpose filled the air like a tangible force. It was as though the very essence of our beings had merged into one, a singular entity driven by a shared desire to change the world for the better.

With our alliance forged and our resolve unyielding, Thalion and I set off into the night, our hearts ablaze with the promise of a brighter future.

For we knew that no matter what lay ahead, we would face it together, united in our quest for justice and liberation.

Alliance in the Making

The dense canopy of the forest enveloped us as we ventured deeper into the heart of the wilderness, leaving the hustle and bustle of Arcadia behind. The only noises in the air were the rustling of leaves and the infrequent chirping of birds. The air was heavy with the smell of pine and earth.

With each step we took, I could feel the weight of our mission pressing down on me like a burden too heavy to bear. We had set out from the safety of the city, determined to find allies in our fight against the king's tyranny, but the road ahead was fraught with uncertainty and danger.

As we walked, I stole a glance at Thalion, whose expression was a mask of determination and resolve. He was the fey prince, burdened with the weight of his responsibilities, yet he bore it with a grace and strength that I found both admirable and intimidating.

Suddenly, our journey was interrupted by the appearance of a group of wary forest nymphs, their ethereal forms blending seamlessly with the foliage around them. They eyed us with suspicion and distrust, their gaze cold and unwelcoming as they assessed us from head to toe.

Thalion stepped forward, his movements deliberate as he attempted to reason with the forest nymphs. His words were measured and diplomatic, his tone gentle yet persuasive as he tried to convince them of our shared goal of overthrowing the corrupt king.

But the forest nymphs remained unmoved, their distrust evident in the way they crossed their arms over their chests and narrowed their eyes at us. They were creatures of the forest, wary of outsiders and protective of their home, and no amount of persuasion seemed to sway them.

Frustration bubbled up inside me as I watched Thalion's efforts fall on deaf ears. We needed allies if we were to stand any chance against the king's enforcers, and the forest nymphs were our best hope of finding them. But if they refused to listen to reason, what hope did we have of convincing anyone else to join our cause?

With a heavy sigh, I stepped forward to stand beside Thalion, my heart pounding in my chest as I prepared to make one last attempt to sway the forest nymphs to our side. We had come too far to turn back now, and failure was not an option.

Taking a deep breath, I met the gaze of the forest nymphs head-on, my voice steady as I spoke. "Our worlds may be different, but we have a common enemy," I stated, my voice resonating through the forest's stillness. "The king's tyranny knows no limits; we will surely fall apart if we fail to stand together."

For a moment, the forest nymphs remained silent, their expressions unreadable as they considered my words. And then, slowly but surely, their resistance began to crumble, replaced by a glimmer of hope and determination.

With a nod of agreement, the forest nymphs stepped aside, allowing us to pass. It was a small victory, but it filled me with a renewed sense of determination and purpose. We may have encountered resistance along the way, but we were not alone in our fight against the king's tyranny. And with each ally we gained, our chances of victory grew stronger.

The dense foliage of the forest enveloped us, casting dappled shadows across the forest floor as we pressed on, determined to prove ourselves to the wary forest nymphs. Despite Thalion's best efforts at diplomacy, the nymphs remained unmoved, their eyes still filled with suspicion and doubt. It was clear that they would not be swayed easily.

Undeterred by their skepticism, we continued our journey deeper into the heart of the forest, our determination unwavering despite the obstacles that lay ahead. With every step we took, the tension in the air grew, and the only sounds to break the silence were the occasional hoot of an owl and the rustle of leaves.

As we rounded a bend in the path, we stumbled upon a pack of fearsome werewolves, their snarling forms blocking our path and demanding to know our business in the forest. My heart leaped into my throat at the sight of them, their sharp teeth gleaming in the dappled sunlight as they advanced on us with predatory intent.

With a proud and erect stance, Thalion moved up to speak with the pack leader. Despite the terror that was nibbling at the borders of my thoughts, he added, "We mean you no harm," in a firm voice. "We are simply passing through on our way to seek allies in our fight against the king's tyranny."

The werewolf leader regarded us with a wary eye, his gaze flickering between Thalion and me as though assessing our worth. "And what makes you think we would be willing to help you?" he growled, his voice low and menacing.

Thalion's jaw clenched, his gaze unwavering as he met the werewolf leader's stare. "Because we share a common enemy," he said, his voice firm with conviction. "The king's enforcers seek to eradicate all magical beings from the realm, regardless of race or allegiance. If we do not stand together, we will surely fall apart."

The werewolf leader seemed to consider Thalion's words for a moment, his expression unreadable as he weighed his options. And then, to my surprise, he let out a low growl of acknowledgment and stepped aside, allowing us to pass. Relief flooded through me as we continued on our journey, the tension in the air slowly dissipating as we left the werewolves behind.

It was a small victory, but it filled me with hope that perhaps, just perhaps, we were on the right path after all.

The dense canopy above cast shifting patterns of light and shadow upon the forest floor as we ventured deeper into the heart of the wilderness. With each step, the air grew thicker with tension, but also with an undeniable sense of camaraderie that seemed to bind Thalion and me together.

As we walked, Thalion and I found ourselves sharing stories of our pasts, our hopes and fears laid bare in the quiet stillness of the forest. I spoke of my childhood in Arcadia, of the struggles I faced as a young witch in a world that feared and mistrusted magic. Thalion, in turn, shared tales of his life in the fey kingdom, of the responsibilities he carried as a prince and the expectations that weighed upon him like a heavy cloak.

Despite the darkness of our pasts, there was a sense of catharsis in sharing our stories with one another, a feeling of release that washed over us like a cleansing tide. For the first time in as long as I could remember, I felt truly seen and understood, and it filled me with a sense of belonging that I had never known before.

As we walked, our laughter echoed through the trees like a song, filling the air with a sense of lightness and joy that seemed to banish the shadows that lurked in the corners of my mind. In that moment, it felt as though nothing else mattered but the here and now, and the bond that had formed between Thalion and me.

But even as we reveled in each other's company, we knew that the dangers of the forest still lurked around every corner, waiting to strike when we least expected it. We had come too far to turn back now, and the road ahead was fraught with uncertainty and peril.

With each step we took, our bond grew stronger, our shared experiences forging a connection that transcended mere friendship. In each other, we found solace and strength, and it was that bond that would carry us through the trials that lay ahead.

As the sun dipped below the horizon and the forest grew cloaked in darkness, Thalion and I pressed on, our hearts filled with a sense of determination and resolve. For no matter what dangers awaited us in the depths of the forest, we knew that together, we were unstoppable.

As the forest enveloped us in a blanket of shadow as we ventured deeper into its heart, the tangled undergrowth and towering trees seeming to close in around us with each step. Despite the darkness that surrounded us, there was a flicker of warmth between Thalion and me, a connection that grew stronger with every shared moment.

As we walked, Thalion and I found ourselves opening up to each other in ways we never thought possible. I spoke of the struggles I faced as a young witch, of the prejudice and fear that had followed me like a shadow throughout my life. Thalion, in turn, shared tales of his life in the fey kingdom, of the expectations placed upon him as a prince and the weight of responsibility that rested upon his shoulders.

With each word we spoke, it felt as though a barrier had been lifted between us, allowing us to see each other more clearly than ever before. Our hopes and fears, our dreams and desires—all laid bare in the quiet stillness of the forest, where no judgment could touch us.

Despite the dangers that lurked in the shadows, there was a sense of peace between us, a feeling of safety that came from knowing we were not alone in our struggles. In each other, we found solace and strength, and it was that bond that carried us through the darkest of times.

As we walked, our laughter echoed through the trees like a song, filling the air with a sense of lightness and joy that seemed to banish the darkness that lurked in the corners of our minds. In those moments, it felt as though nothing else mattered but the here and now, and the connection that had formed between us.

But even as we reveled in each other's company, we knew that the dangers of the forest still lurked around every corner, waiting to strike when we least expected it. We had come too far to turn back now, and the road ahead was fraught with uncertainty and peril.

With each step we took, our bond grew stronger, our shared experiences forging a connection that transcended mere friendship. In each other, we found hope and courage, and it was that bond that would carry us through the trials that lay ahead. As the darkness of night descended upon the forest, Thalion and I pressed on, our hearts filled with a sense of determination and resolve.

The dense foliage of the forest began to thin as we ventured deeper into its heart, the tangled undergrowth giving way to open meadows and rolling hills. The air was heavy with the scent of wildflowers and pine, and for a moment, it felt as though the weight of the world had been lifted from our shoulders.

But even as we reveled in the beauty of our surroundings, we knew that our journey was far from over. The true test of our alliance still lay ahead, and we could not afford to let our guard down for even a moment.

With renewed determination, Seraphina and I pressed on, our hearts set on our ultimate goal of uniting magical beings from all corners of the realm against the corrupt king. As we reached the edge of the forest and gazed out into the vast expanse beyond, I felt a surge of anticipation course through my veins. The world stretched out before us like a vast canvas waiting to be painted, and I knew that our actions in the days to come would shape the course of history.

But despite the challenges that lay ahead, I took comfort in the knowledge that Seraphina was by my side. Together, we were stronger than we could ever be alone, and no matter what obstacles we faced, we would face them together. With a silent nod of understanding, Seraphina and I set off into the unknown, our hearts filled with determination and resolve. No matter what challenges awaited us on the road ahead, we were ready to face them head-on.

Rallying Allies

The air in the witches' hidden enclave was heavy with the scent of moss and magic as Seraphina and I made our way through the dense foliage. The ancient trees towered overhead like silent sentinels guarding their secrets. Wary glances followed us as we approached the clearing where the witches held court, their whispered conversations falling silent as we drew near.

At the heart of the clearing stood a figure cloaked in shadow, her presence commanding respect and awe. This was Elara, the leader of the witches, a formidable woman whose power was matched only by her cunning. As we approached, her piercing gaze fixed upon us, her eyes seeming to see straight into our souls.

"Why have you come here, Seraphina, Thalion?" Elara's voice was like the rustle of leaves on a breeze, soft yet filled with an underlying edge of danger. "What do you seek from us?"

I exchanged a glance with Seraphina, feeling the weight of Elara's scrutiny bearing down upon us. We had rehearsed our speech a dozen times on our journey here, but now that the moment had come, my mind went blank, and I struggled to find the words.

"We seek your aid, Elara," Seraphina spoke up, her voice steady despite the tension that hung in the air. "We seek to overthrow the tyrant who rules over our land with an iron fist, to restore peace and justice to our people."

Elara's expression remained unreadable as she listened to Seraphina's words, her gaze flickering with a hint of amusement. "And why should we help you?" she asked, her voice laced with skepticism. "What makes you think we would risk our lives for the sake of strangers?"

I took a step forward, meeting Elara's gaze with a steely determination of mine. "Because we have seen the injustices inflicted upon our people," I said, my voice ringing out clear and strong. "We have seen the suffering caused by the king's tyranny, and we refuse to stand idly by and watch it continue."

Elara regarded me with a measuring look, her eyes seeming to pierce straight through to my soul. "And what makes you think you can succeed where others have failed?" she asked, her tone challenging.

"We have each other," Seraphina replied, her voice ringing out with unwavering conviction. "We have formed an alliance, united in our determination to see justice done. With your help, we can overthrow the king and restore peace to our land."

The tension in the air was palpable as we waited for Elara's response, her silence stretching on like an eternity as she deliberated our fate. I exchanged a nervous glance with Seraphina, the weight of uncertainty pressing down upon us like a suffocating blanket.

Finally, after what felt like an eternity, Elara spoke, her voice cutting through the tense silence like a knife. "Very well," she said, her tone betraying nothing of her thoughts. "We will hear what you have to say."

Elara's comments struck home for me, and I felt a flood of relief sweep over me like a tidal wave. I let out a breath that I hadn't realized I'd been holding. But even as I breathed a sigh of relief, I knew that our trials were far from over.

Just as I was about to speak, a voice broke through the tension like a ray of sunlight piercing through storm clouds. It was Lysandra, a young witch whose fiery spirit was loud enough to be heard by the deaf, her eyes blazing with determination as she stepped forward to join our cause. "I stand with Seraphina and Thalion," Lysandra declared, her voice ringing out clear and strong. "I will fight alongside them to overthrow the king and restore peace to our land."

A ripple of murmurs swept through the gathered witches, their expressions ranging from uncertainty to outright hostility. But Lysandra stood firm, her gaze never wavering as she faced down the skeptics and doubters. Inspired by Lysandra's bravery, other witches began to step forward, their voices joining hers in a chorus of support. One by one, they pledged their allegiance to our cause, their murmurs of agreement growing louder with each passing moment.

I felt a surge of gratitude welling up inside me as I looked around at the faces of our newfound allies, their determination mirrored in the depths of their eyes. Despite the challenges that lay ahead, I knew that we were not alone—that together, we would stand strong against the forces of tyranny and oppression.

With our alliance forged and our resolve unyielding, Seraphina and I set out once more into the night, our hearts ablaze with the promise of a brighter future. The journey to seek the fey's support was fraught with peril, each step bringing Seraphina and me deeper into the heart of the fey kingdom where shadows danced among the ancient trees like specters of the past. We tread carefully, wary of attracting the attention of the fey, whose reputation for capriciousness and cunning preceded them.

As we entered the hallowed groves where the fey made their home, a sense of unease settled over me like a heavy cloak. The air crackled with magic, and I could feel the eyes of unseen watchers following our every move.

At the heart of the grove stood the fey queen's court, a glittering spectacle of ethereal beauty and otherworldly splendor. The fey moved with a grace and elegance that seemed to defy the laws of nature, their voices lilting and melodious as they danced among the moonlit shadows.

At the center of it all sat Queen Titania, a vision of regal elegance and aloof detachment. Her eyes, a piercing shade of emerald green, bore into me with a scrutiny that made my skin crawl, as if she could see straight through the facade I had built around myself.

I swallowed hard, forcing myself to meet Titania's gaze with a steely resolve. "Your Majesty," I said, my voice steady despite the tremors of fear that threatened to consume me. "We come seeking your aid in our fight against the king's tyranny."

Titania regarded me with a cool detachment, her lips curling into a faint smile that sent shivers down my spine. "And what makes you think that I would aid you in your quest?" she asked, her voice like honey laced with poison.

I glanced at Seraphina, her expression mirroring my own uncertainty as we searched for the right words to sway the fey queen to our cause. "Because we share a common enemy," I said finally, my voice ringing out clear and strong. "The king seeks to oppress all magical beings, fey, and human alike. We cannot stand idly by and watch as he destroys everything we hold dear."

Titania's smile widened, her eyes flickering with a hint of amusement. "You speak with conviction, young prince," she said, her voice tinged with a note of mockery. "But words alone are not enough to earn my support. What do you offer in return for my aid?"

I hesitated, knowing that promises or pleas did not easily sway the fey. But then, an idea struck me—a gamble, but one worth taking if it meant securing the fey's support in our fight against the king.

I knelt before Titania, my head bowed in a gesture of deference. "I offer you my allegiance, Queen Titania," I said, my voice ringing out loud and clear. "I swear to fight alongside the fey in your quest for freedom, to stand by your side in times of need and adversity."

A murmur rippled through the fey court at my words, their eyes widening in surprise at my boldness. But Titania remained unmoved, her expression betraying nothing of her thoughts as she regarded me with a cool detachment.

Finally, after what felt like an eternity, Titania spoke, her voice echoing through the silent grove like a whisper in the wind. "Very well, Prince Thalion," she said, her tone betraying a hint of satisfaction. "You have shown courage and conviction in the face of adversity. I shall consider your offer, and if it pleases me, I shall grant you the aid you seek."

The atmosphere in Queen Titania's court was thick with tension, every eye fixed on Thalion and me as we awaited the fey queen's verdict. Titania's gaze bore into us like a pair of icy daggers, her expression inscrutable as she deliberated our fate.

I could feel the weight of her scrutiny pressing down on me, a suffocating pressure that threatened to crush my resolve. But I refused to back down, meeting Titania's piercing gaze with a defiant stare of my own.

"We seek only to right the wrongs that have been inflicted upon our kind," I said, my voice steady despite the turmoil churning inside me. "We ask for your aid in our fight against the king's tyranny, not out of greed or ambition, but out of a desire for justice and freedom."

Titania's lips curled into a faint smile, her eyes gleaming with a hint of amusement. "You are bold, mortal," she said, her voice like the rustle of leaves on the wind. "But boldness alone will not win you my support. You must prove yourselves worthy of it."

Before I could respond, a voice rang out from the crowd—a voice filled with determination and conviction. I turned to see a young fey prince named Eirik stepping forward, his eyes blazing with defiance as he addressed Queen Titania.

"Your Majesty," he said, his voice ringing out clear and strong. "I have seen firsthand the suffering inflicted upon our kind by the king's enforcers. I cannot stand idly by and watch as our people are oppressed and persecuted. I pledge my support to Seraphina and Thalion's cause, and I urge my fellow fey to do the same."

As the throng fell silent in agreement, fey of all sizes and forms came forward to join Eirik in swearing loyalty. Despite Titania's cool detachment, I could see a flicker of uncertainty in her eyes—a crack in the facade of her regal composure.

Slowly but surely, the fey began to rally to our cause, their voices rising in a chorus of defiance against the king's tyranny. I felt a surge of hope welling up inside me, a glimmer of light in the darkness that threatened to consume us all.

With each fey that pledged their support, our coalition grew stronger, and our resolve became more steadfast. And as we stood there in the heart of the fey kingdom, surrounded by allies old and new, I knew that together, we would be unstoppable.

As we moved out of the fey kingdom, the road stretched out before us like an endless ribbon of dust and dirt, winding our way through unfamiliar lands and treacherous terrain. Seraphina and I rode side by side, our hearts heavy with the weight of our mission but our spirits buoyed by the knowledge that we were not alone.

Our first stop was the hidden sanctuary of the dryads, ancient guardians of the forests who had long since retreated from the world of mortals. Deep within the heart of the densest woodland, we found their grove—a tranquil oasis untouched by the ravages of time.

As we entered the sacred glade, we were greeted by a chorus of rustling leaves emerged from the shadows and covered us, it dragged us to the heart of the grove as if by magic. The dryads emerged from the shadows filling the square, their forms ethereal and otherworldly as they regarded us with solemn curiosity.

Their leader, an ancient dryad known as Gaia, sat on his throne gazing at us, her eyes wise and understanding as she listened to our tale of woe. We spoke of the king's tyranny, of the suffering inflicted upon magical beings by his cruel reign, and of our quest to unite the realms against him.

But Gaia was unmoved, her expression impassive as she considered our words. The dryads were creatures of the forest, bound to their ancient groves by an unbreakable bond, and they had little interest in mortals' affairs.

Undeterred, Seraphina and I pleaded our case with all the eloquence and passion we could muster, appealing to the dryads' sense of duty and honor. We spoke of the beauty of the natural world, of the delicate balance that existed between all living things, and of the dire consequences that would follow if the king's tyranny was allowed to continue unchecked.

Slowly but surely, Gaia's demeanor began to soften, her eyes growing thoughtful as she contemplated our words. At last, she nodded solemnly, her voice like the whisper of leaves on the wind.

"We will stand with you," she said, her words carrying the weight of centuries of wisdom. "Not out of obligation or duty, but out of a deep-seated belief in the sanctity of life and the importance of protecting those who cannot protect themselves."

With the support of the dryads secured, Seraphina and I set out once more, our hearts lightened by the knowledge that we were one step closer to achieving our goal. But our journey was far from over, and many challenges still lay ahead.

Our next stop was the hidden realm of the merfolk, an ancient civilization that dwelled beneath the waves. Guided by a mystical artifact given to us by Gaia, we plunged into the depths of the ocean, our lungs burning with the need for air as we descended into the darkness below.

At last, we reached the fabled city of Atlantis, a shimmering metropolis of coral and pearl that glowed with an otherworldly light and mesmerizing glow. The merfolk greeted us with a mixture of curiosity and suspicion, their webbed hands clutching tridents and spears as they regarded us with wary eyes.

The merfolk ruler, King Nereus, greeted us with a mixture of awe and skepticism. His regal demeanor was softened by the weight of responsibility that rested upon his shoulders. As he listened, we recounted our struggles against the king's tyranny, our voices echoing through the grand halls of the palace.

But even as we spoke, I could sense the doubt lingering in King Nereus' eyes—a doubt born from centuries of isolation and mistrust. The merfolk had long remained hidden from the surface world, their secrets guarded fiercely against outsiders.

Yet despite the odds stacked against us, we refused to back down, our resolve unyielding in the face of adversity. Slowly but surely, we began to earn the trust of the merfolk, our words and actions proving our sincerity and our commitment to their plight. We shared stories of our past victories and our hopes for the future, our voices rising above the roar of the ocean as we spoke of unity and solidarity.

As the day went by, we worked tirelessly alongside the merfolk, training together and preparing for the battle that would decide the fate of the realm. Together, we forged weapons of enchanted coral and pearl, imbued with the magic of the ocean depths. With the merfolk at our side, we knew that victory was within our grasp and that together, we would usher in a new era of peace and prosperity for all who called the realm home.

Strengthening Bonds

The moon was low in the sky, bathing the secret alcove where Seraphina and Thalion had spent the night in a silvery glow. The first rays of sunlight filtered through the dense canopy of trees overhead. Seraphina and I exchanged a silent nod as we prepared for the journey ahead, our resolve unwavering in the face of uncertainty.

With our supplies packed and our weapons at the ready, we set out into the wilderness, the path ahead shrouded in mystery and danger. Every rustle of leaves and snap of twigs set my nerves on edge, but I pushed aside my fear, focusing instead on the task at hand. As we ventured deeper into the forest's heart, the air grew heavy with the scent of earth and moss, and the sounds of the outside world faded into the background. We moved in silence, our senses alert for any sign of danger that might lie in wait.

Hours passed in tense anticipation, until finally, we reached our destination—a clearing bathed in dappled sunlight, where the king's forces had been rumored to gather. Taking cover behind a thicket of bushes, we watched and waited, our hearts pounding in unison.

At last, our patience was rewarded as a group of soldiers emerged from the trees, their armor glinting in the sunlight as they marched in formation. With bated breath, we observed their movements, noting their numbers and weapons.

But as we prepared to make our escape, disaster struck—a branch snapped beneath Seraphina's foot, the sound echoing through the forest like a thunderclap. In an instant, all eyes were upon us, and we knew that our cover had been compromised.

With a silent curse, I grabbed Seraphina's hand and broke into a run, weaving through the trees with all the speed and agility we possessed. Arrows whistled through the air around us, but we pressed on, driven by desperation and determination.

At last, we reached the safety of an ancient chamber, our chests heaving with exertion as we collapsed onto the forest floor. We had narrowly escaped capture, but we knew that our ordeal was far from over.

With the king's forces hot on our trail, we had no choice but to keep moving, our quest for justice and freedom driving us ever onward into the unknown. As we disappeared into the depths of the forest once more, I knew that no matter what trials awaited us, Seraphina and I would face them together, united in our shared purpose and unbreakable bond.

As we entered the dimly lit chamber, the tension that had gripped us on the chase slowly began to melt away, replaced by a sense of peace and tranquility. Seraphina collapsed onto the threadbare cot, exhaustion etched into every line of her face, and I couldn't help but feel a surge of protectiveness wash over me.

Without a word, I joined her on the cot, pulling her into my arms and holding her close as we sought solace in each other's embrace and basked in the glow of our feelings. In the warmth of the firelight, I traced the lines of her face with gentle fingertips, committing every curve and contour to memory.

The darkness of the night enveloped us like a thick blanket, casting shadows that danced across the walls of our sanctuary. Seraphina and I lay side by side, the faint flicker of candlelight casting a warm glow over her features as she slept soundly beside me. Despite the chaos of the world outside, in this moment, there was only peace.

But even in the stillness of the night, the echoes of our pasts lingered like ghosts, haunting us with memories of battles fought and lost. I turned to Seraphina, her face relaxed in sleep, and felt a surge of protectiveness wash over me. She had faced so much already, and yet here she was, still standing, still fighting. It filled me with a sense of awe and admiration that I could scarcely put into words.

With a gentle touch, I brushed a strand of hair away from Seraphina's face, tracing the line of her jaw with careful fingertips. In the dim light, she seemed almost ethereal, a vision of strength and beauty that took my breath away. And yet, beneath the surface, I knew that she carried wounds that ran deep, scars left by years of struggle and hardship.

As I watched Seraphina sleep, a surge of emotion welled up inside me, threatening to overwhelm me with its intensity. I reached out and took her hand in mine, feeling the warmth of her touch seep into my skin like sunlight breaking through the clouds. In that moment, I knew that no matter what trials lay ahead, as long as we faced them together, we could overcome anything.

With a sense of determination burning bright within me, I leaned in and pressed a gentle kiss to Seraphina's forehead, silently reaffirming my commitment to her and to our cause. We would never be alone as long as we had each other, I realized as I lay there next to her and felt the constant rise and fall of her chest against my

fingers.

A warm glow filled the room as the first rays of morning peaked through the window, waking Seraphina, who was stirring next to me, her eyelids fluttering awake. She smiled up at me, her gaze filled with warmth and affection, and I couldn't help but return the gesture.

"Good morning," she murmured, her voice soft and melodic, like the sound of a distant waterfall. "Did you sleep well?"

I nodded, unable to tear my gaze away from her. "Better than I have in years," I admitted, feeling a weight lift from my shoulders with each passing moment. "And you?"

Seraphina's smile widened, her eyes shining with a hint of mischief. "Like a babe in its mother's arms," she replied, her voice tinged with amusement. "But enough about that. We have work to do."

I nodded, pushing aside the lingering traces of sleep as I sat up and swung my legs over the edge of the cot. "You're right," I agreed, my mind already turning to the challenges that lay ahead. "We can't afford to rest on our laurels. Not now, not ever."

Together, Seraphina and I rose from the cot and made our way to the training grounds, our footsteps echoing in the silence of the early morning. As we sparred with wooden swords and practiced our spells, I couldn't help but feel a sense of pride swell within me. We were warriors, forged in the fires of adversity and bound together by a love that defied all odds.

As we honed our skills and sharpened our resolve, I knew that no matter what trials lay ahead, as long as we faced them together, we would emerge victorious. We had come so far together and faced so many trials and tribulations, and yet the distance between us seemed to grow with each passing day. It weighed heavily on my heart, this sense of uncertainty and doubt that lingered between us like a shadow, casting a pall over even the brightest of moments.

But despite our differences, I knew that there was still common ground to be found, a shared purpose that bound us together even in the darkest of times. And so, as we walked side by side through the forest, I reached out and took Seraphina's hand in mine, a silent gesture of solidarity and support.

She glanced up at me, her eyes shimmering with unspoken emotion, and for a moment, it felt as though the world around us had faded away, leaving only the two of us standing alone in the darkness. At that moment, I knew that no matter what challenges lay ahead, we could overcome anything if we faced them together.

As we continued our journey, the tension between us seemed to ease, replaced by a sense of warmth and camaraderie that had been missing for far too long. We talked and laughed like old friends, sharing stories and memories as we walked, our footsteps echoing through the silent forest.

And in those fleeting moments of peace and companionship, I felt something stir within me, a longing that I couldn't quite name. It was as though a part of me had been awakened, a part that had long lain dormant beneath the weight of duty and responsibility.

But as much as I wanted to lose myself in the warmth of Seraphina's presence, I knew that there were still battles to be fought and that our time together was fleeting at best. And so, with a heavy heart, I forced myself to push aside my doubts and fears, focusing instead on the task at hand.

But even as we pressed on, the memory of our shared moments lingered like a bittersweet melody, haunting me with its beauty and sorrow. For in those stolen moments of tenderness and passion, I had glimpsed a future that seemed just out of reach, a future where Seraphina and I could be together without fear or hesitation.

But for now, all I could do was cherish the time we had together, knowing that each moment was a precious gift that could be taken from us at any time. And so, as we walked through the forest, hand in hand, I made a silent vow to cherish every moment, to hold onto the memory of our love even in the darkest of times.

For in the end, it was love that would sustain us, love that would give us the strength to face whatever trials lay ahead, and love that would light the way through the darkness. And as long as we had that, I knew that nothing could ever truly tear us apart.

The Final Stand

The air was thick with tension as we stood at the edge of the battlefield, surrounded by allies from every corner of the realm. Witches, fey, werewolves, and creatures of all kinds gathered around us, their eyes reflecting the flickering light of the torches that lined the field.

The king's army loomed on the horizon, a dark mass of soldiers, beasts, and sorcerers, their banners fluttering in the wind as they advanced with grim determination. Fear gripped my heart like a vice as I watched them draw nearer, their numbers seemingly endless.

Beside me, Thalion stood tall and resolute, his jaw set in a firm line as he surveyed the enemy ranks. His hand tightened around the hilt of his sword, his knuckles white with tension, but his eyes burned with a fierce determination that sent a shiver down my spine.

"We can do this," he said, his voice low but steady. "We have to."

I nodded, my own resolve hardening as I met his gaze. Together, we had faced countless trials and tribulations, but this would be our greatest challenge yet. We were the last hope for the realm, and its fate rested with us.

As the king's army drew closer, a sense of urgency swept through the ranks of our allies. Witches muttered incantations under their breath, their hands glowing with arcane energy. Fey danced through the air, their movements graceful yet deadly as they prepared to unleash their powers upon the enemy.

The ground trembled beneath our feet as the first wave of the king's forces crashed against our defenses. Swords clashed, spells crackled through the air, and the sound of battle filled the night, a cacophony of screams and shouts that echoed across the field.

Thalion leaped into the fray, his sword flashing in the moonlight as he cut through the enemy ranks with skill and precision. I followed close behind, my own magic crackling around me as I unleashed blasts of fire and lightning upon our foes.

I followed close behind, my own magic burning bright as I unleashed a devastating spell that sent shockwaves rippling through the enemy lines. Together, we fought with a ferocity born of desperation, our love and our resolve shining bright amidst the darkness of war.

But despite our best efforts, the king's forces seemed endless, their ranks bolstered by powerful sorcerers and monstrous beasts. For every enemy we struck down, two more seemed to take their place, their determination to crush the rebellion evident in their eyes.

With a grim determination, I summoned the last reserves of my strength, weaving intricate patterns of light and shadow around me as I prepared to face the king in one final showdown. Every fiber of my being thrummed with energy, my heart pounding in my chest as I steeled myself for the battle ahead.

The king's gaze locked with mine, his eyes burning with malice as he raised his hand, a ball of dark energy forming in his palm. Without hesitation, I unleashed a barrage of spells, my magic colliding with his in a dazzling display of light and shadow.

The ground trembled beneath us as our powers clashed, the air crackling with energy as we fought for control of the battlefield. Thalion fought at my side, his sword flashing in the dim light as he cut down enemy soldiers with a ferocity born of desperation.

But even as we fought, I could feel the king's power growing stronger with each passing moment, his dark magic swirling around him like a cloak of shadows. With a mighty roar, he charged forward, his eyes fixed on Thalion as he prepared to strike the killing blow.

I stepped forward to intercept him, my own sword raised high as I prepared to face him in single combat. Our blades clashed with a deafening roar, the sound of metal on metal echoing through the air like a death knell.

With every strike, I could feel the weight of the king's power pressing down upon me, threatening to overwhelm me with its sheer intensity. But I refused to yield, my determination unwavering as I fought with every ounce of strength and skill I possessed.

Beside me, Thalion fought with a courage born of desperation, his sword flashing in the dim light as he danced around the king's attacks. With a mighty swing, he struck a blow against the king's defenses, his sword biting deep into the king's armor.

But even as the king staggered, his resolve remained unbroken. With a roar of rage, he unleashed a torrent of dark energy, his power engulfing us like a tidal wave. I felt myself being swept away, my vision swimming as I struggled to maintain my footing.

And then, just when it seemed like all hope was lost, I felt a surge of energy coursing through me, my powers igniting like a beacon of light in the darkness. With a defiant cry, I unleashed a devastating spell, my magic tearing through the king's defenses like a bolt of lightning.

The king staggered, his dark magic flickering and fading as he fell to his knees before us. With a final roar of defiance, he raised his sword high, preparing to strike one last desperate blow.

But before he could act, Thalion was upon him, his sword flashing in the dim light as he struck the killing blow. With a mighty roar, the king fell, his dark magic dissipating like smoke in the wind, and his body turned into a pile of sand and dissipated.

The battlefield fell silent, the cries of the wounded echoing through the air like a dirge. Thalion and I stood amidst the ruins of the battlefield, our hearts heavy with the weight of the sacrifices that had been made. But even as we mourned, I felt a sense of hope stirring within me, a glimmer of light amidst the darkness. With the king defeated and his forces scattered, the realm was ours once more.

Seraphina moved among the wounded, her every step a testament to her unwavering resolve. Her hands glowed with a soft, soothing light as she tended to the injured, her magic weaving through their bodies to ease their pain and hasten their healing. Despite the exhaustion etched into the lines of her face, she showed no signs of faltering, her determination to ease their suffering driving her forward with every passing moment.

I stood watch over the fallen, my sword held aloft in a silent vow to protect them at all costs. My eyes scanned the horizon, searching for any sign of danger that might threaten us in our moment of vulnerability. Every rustle of the wind, every distant sound sent a shiver down my spine, my senses heightened by the lingering adrenaline of battle.

The weight of responsibility pressed down upon me like a leaden cloak, each fallen comrade a painful reminder of the sacrifices that had been made. But I refused to yield to despair, to let the darkness consume me. I had sworn an oath to protect my people, and I would honor that oath with every fiber of my being.

As I stood vigil over the battlefield, my thoughts drifted to Seraphina—my partner in both love and war. Her courage and compassion had been a guiding light in the darkest of times, her presence a source of strength that had sustained me through the fiercest of battles. In her, I had found not only a lover but a true companion, someone with whom I could share the burden of leadership and the weight of responsibility.

Despite the horrors that surrounded us, there was a sense of peace in that moment, a quiet calm that settled over the battlefield like a blanket of stars. The cries of the wounded faded into the distance, replaced by the steady rhythm of our breathing and the soft rustle of the wind through the trees.

But even as we tended to the wounded and stood watch over the fallen, I knew that our work was far from over. The battle may have been won, but the war still raged on, its flames fueled by the hatred and greed of those who sought to seize power for themselves.

We had emerged victorious, but the scars of war would linger long after the last sword had fallen silent. And yet, in that moment, as Seraphina and I stood side by side amidst the ruins of the battlefield, I knew that together, we would face whatever trials lay ahead. For our love was a beacon of hope in the darkness, a light that would guide us through even the darkest of nights.

A New Dawn

As the sun rose to welcome the new day, the first rays of dawn slowly emerged from behind the horizon, illuminating the sky in shades of orange and gold. Seraphina and I stood together amidst the ruins of the battlefield, and our eyes turned towards the eastern sky, where the promise of a new beginning awaited us.

The air was cool and crisp, carrying with it the scent of fresh earth. Despite the tranquility of the morning, there was a heaviness that lingered in the air, a tangible reminder of the sacrifices that had been made in the name of freedom and justice.

As the first rays of sunlight washed over us, Seraphina and I shared a moment of silent reflection, our hearts heavy with the weight of the lives that had been lost. Each fallen comrade was a testament to the cost of war, a reminder of the price that had been paid for our victory.

Together, we stood in silent tribute to those who had given their lives in the fight for freedom, our hearts heavy with the weight of their sacrifice. Each gravestone was a reminder of the cost of war, a solemn testament to the bravery and heroism of those who had gone before us.

As we paid our respects to the fallen, I felt a swell of emotion rise within me—a mixture of sorrow for the lives lost and gratitude for the sacrifices made. Each gravestone was a testament to the bravery and heroism of those who had given their lives in the fight against tyranny. And yet, amidst the sorrow, there was also a sense of hope—a belief that their sacrifice had not been in vain, that their memory would live on in the hearts of those they had left behind.

With heavy hearts and a renewed sense of purpose, Seraphina and I turned our attention to the task of rebuilding our shattered world. With the support of our allies, we began the arduous process of clearing away the debris and laying the groundwork for a new era of peace and prosperity.

Together, Seraphina and I worked tirelessly, our hands joined together as we labored side by side to bring about positive change. Despite the enormity of the task before us, our determination remained unshaken. We were aware that every stone placed and every beam raised brought us one step closer to achieving our goal of a better future.

As we worked, Seraphina and I shared moments of tenderness and passion, our love grows stronger with each passing day. In the quiet moments between tasks, we stole away to be alone, our hands and hearts united in a shared bond that transcended words.

In those moments, as we held each other close, I felt a sense of peace wash over me—a sense that no matter what trials lay ahead, as long as we were together, we could face them head-on. For in Seraphina's arms, I found solace and strength, her love a guiding light in the darkness that surrounded us.

As the days turned into weeks and the weeks into months, our world began to take shape once more. The war's scars gradually started to disappear, to be replaced by the hope of a better future.

From our vantage point, we could see the fruits of our labor spread out before us—the bustling streets filled with merchants and travelers, the fields teeming with crops ready for harvest, and the once-ruined buildings now restored to their former glory. It was a sight that filled us both with pride and a sense of accomplishment, knowing that we had played a part in rebuilding our shattered world.

But amidst the celebrations and the joyous cries of the people below, there lingered a sense of solemnity—a reminder of the sacrifices that had been made in the fight for freedom. As we watched the revelry unfold, Seraphina's hand found mine, her touch a silent reassurance in the midst of the chaos.

"We've come a long way, haven't we?" she said, her voice soft with emotion.

I nodded, unable to find the words to express the depth of my gratitude for everything she had done. In that moment, as we stood together beneath the stars, I knew that no matter what challenges lay ahead, as long as Seraphina was by my side, we could face them together.

As the night wore on, the sounds of music and laughter filled the air, echoing off the stone walls of the castle and mingling with the gentle rustle of the wind. Seraphina and I joined in the festivities, our hearts light with the knowledge that we had brought peace and prosperity to our kingdom once more.

Amidst the revelry, we found ourselves drawn to each other, our steps falling into sync as we danced beneath the stars. In that moment, as our eyes met and our bodies moved as one, I felt a sense of peace wash over me—a feeling of completeness that I had never known before.

"I love you," Seraphina whispered, her voice barely audible above the music.

"I love you too," I replied, my heart overflowing with emotion.

Together, we danced until the early hours of the morning, our laughter ringing out across the courtyard as we celebrated our victory and the new dawn that awaited us. As the first light of dawn began to creep over the horizon, I knew that no matter what trials lay ahead, as long as Seraphina was by my side, we could face them together. For our love was a force more powerful than any magic, a bond that could withstand the tests of time and the trials of fate.

THE END